He Doesn't Hurt People Anymore

Also by Dane Swan

Bending the Continuum
A Mingus Lullaby
Tuesday

# HE DOESN'T HURT PEOPLE ANYMORE

## STORIES

# DANE SWAN

DUMA GRAD
CITY OF WORDS

HE DOESN'T HURT PEOPLE ANYMORE
Dane Swan
© 2017 Dane Swan
All rights reserved.

Dumagrad: A City of Words
Toronto, Canada
dumagrad.com
info@dumagrad.com

Hand Wraps originally published by Broken Pencil. Rastavarius originally published online by Tracer Publishing.

Author photo © 2017 by Liz Gallo

Printed and bound in Canada

Library and Archives Canada Cataloguing in Publication

Swan, Dane
[Short stories. Selections]
   He doesn't hurt people anymore : stories / Dane Swan.

ISBN 978-0-9937909-9-7 (softcover)

   I. Title. II. Title: He does not hurt people anymore.

PS8637.W36A6 2017          C813'.6          C2017-902970-3

With thanks to
Dan D'Onorio, Anna Saini, Liz Gallo and Netta Kornberg

# Contents

## Hand Wraps

All these people in this gym. You would think that they would know the basics. Whether it's the boxercisers, or the fresh meat amateurs, when it's my time to teach them, I ask them to show me everything.

"Let me see your jab!

Let me see your cross!

Now one-two!

One-two!

Again!

Again!

Keep your guard up!

You! You just got hit with a hook 'cause your guard is garbage!

If you punch like that you'll break your wrists!

Snap those jabs!

Again!"

And that's before we put the wraps on. If I don't know a face I pull them aside. Ask them to show me how they wrap their hands. We sit down, face-to-face. I watch. The ladies there for fitness classes always get it wrong – so do some of the men. I take their hand into my hands. Slowly unwrap their hands and explain, "Wrapping your knuckles might stop your knuckle from being scratched by the glove, but it doesn't protect your hand. We wrap our hands to protect them."

After unwrapping their mess I explain, "First, we wrap the wrist to protect all the bones in it." After pulling the wraps snugly around their wrists twice I continue. "Then we protect each individual knuckle." I slowly cross-wrap between each finger. "Finally, we tighten up the wrap then go across the knuckles and wrist." It should feel tight. The boxer – and we're using the term lightly here for most of them – should feel like the small bones in their hands are held into place.

I then ask them to wrap their second hand. Most people get it, or just make small mistakes that I immediately fix, but some women like when I hold their hands – what can I say. With everyone's hands properly wrapped, I ask them to shadow box. Not how they imagine they should shadow box, but how if they got into a fight themselves they would shadow box.

Some of these people. Seriously, that's how you're going to protect yourself? Others have pretty impressive form. I take my time. Walk around each fighter and make corrections. Every few minutes I cry out, "Always be circling! What are you always doin'?"

"Circling!" they better scream back, if they don't want to do pushups. There's a reason why poets use boxing as a metaphor for life. It all starts with the footwork.

I can tell who's here to become a boxer and who should be here to become a boxer by studying how they circle their imaginary ring. How they cut off their imaginary opponent's path. The efficiency of their movement.

A boxer can only move in two ways: small compact steps, and large leaping steps. Boxers who use small steps are usually conservative people. They use a tight guard because they understand that they will get touched. It's a safe style for boxers adverse to risk.

The boxers who primarily leap are constantly at risk for being knocked out. They gamble that with speed, they won't be clocked jumping into the fray – adding their forward momentum to their opponent's approaching fist. On the way out of danger, it's a similar problem. Leaping out, they have no way of making small adjustments to avoid being struck. I find myself pushing them to the ground, or slapping them to show them how poor their balance is. Sometimes I'll tell them to never leap in with their head on a straight line.

Ideally, boxers should have footwork that borrows from both ideas. Small steps for a sense of control, and larger steps to add elements of surprise to their game. So few of these bums understand the importance of balance.

It's all one way, or all the other way. After watching and critiquing for ten minutes I put on whatever music pisses them off the most and we start the aerobics class.

Amateurs and these guys is the closest I get to the ring nowadays. Maybe one day one of the kids I work with will become something. But this pays the bills. Show me a gym that doesn't let bums train and I'll show you a gym not making money. There are only so many Wildcard gyms. The rest of us have to diversify. For some that's coaching MMA fighters on the side, for me it's this. Two hours everyday of beautiful women and unhealthy, uncoordinated men bouncing around my gym.

We always do this part to music. These people have a drum beating in the middle of their chests and they still have no rhythm. To box you need to know your personal rhythm. By understanding that, you can break your opponent's rhythm. There are clients who come here for months and still can't do jumping jacks to the beat of the music. "Just copy everyone else!" I find myself screaming. Everything to the beat: jacks, running on spot, jumping imaginary rope, throwing combos and circling to the beat.

When we're done, the fitter boxers and clients usually do some type of circuit training. After that, the crowd thins out even more and the fun starts. My boys, some wannabe tough guys who came to the class, and usually a few women who've been clients so long that they've gained confidence with their technique stay behind. I pull out freshly cleaned head guards. Explain to them that all the head guard does is limit cuts and some bruising. The brain damage is still real. I usually pair my smaller amateur fighters with the tough guys to give them some variety and let the ladies pick their partners. I give them all a round in the ring.

What do I care? They've all signed waivers. For some losing a few brain cells is the most excitement they'll get all week. Sitting in a cubicle. Being a yes man for some bitter boss who's a yes man for some other bitter boss. That doesn't matter in the ring. It's a combination of adrenaline and instinct. If they've ingrained my lessons into their soul they survive. Some thrive there and I'm left asking them to enter a tournament. Others freeze; I cut their three minute round short to protect them and pull them aside.

Away from everyone else, we go through what they did wrong. What they need to work on before I let them back in the ring. I usually give them things to practice at home and send them on their way. Might sound cold-hearted of me, but the ring shows no pity. If I want them to come back I can't either – their health is more important than my kindness. No matter how glossy you make it, whether you sell it as fitness or not – this is still boxing. Poor technique could get you killed. They come here because I am honest. Because their health and safety matters to me. Not enough for me to discourage them from trying to fight, but enough to make sure that if they're taking a risk it's a reasonable one.

This doesn't suck. It's far from the glory I felt when I was a successful amateur, or when I turned pro. There's no high like when I was winning smaller belts, or fighting top ten ranked opponents. But there's also no lows like getting knocked out, forgetting my name, being rushed to a hospital because you can't stop throwing up after a brutal fight, getting a cracked rib or breaking a hand. I remember things a lot better now. It'll never all come back. But I'm good. It's a comfortable middle. Sometimes I get lucky, find a decent amateur who does well in tournaments. We take a picture of them with their medals, frame it and put it on the wall, but that's their moment not mine.

When I first started this gym, we were in the basement of a buddy's bar. It was strictly for fighters. I made enough money to move here and then financial responsibility hit. I have a couple employees, real bills, and taxes. I can't do this for personal glory. Things changed but the business survived.

After sparring is done, I brief all my amateurs. If I'm lucky, one of the ladies will ask me to show her how to wrap her hands. If they've been sparring they already know. It's just a subtle way of telling me that they want me to hold their hands – I can dig that.

## Eurydice

"So this is your last day Jevon?" the thirty-something white stock trader asks the black twenty-something drug dealer as they split eggs and bacon in the professional's newly renovated kitchen.

"Yeah Mr. T," the dealer, Jevon, replies between toast and his over-easy eggs. "Thanks for allowing me to store my product in the back of your basement."

"Your money is going to pay my kids' college tuition."

"Yeah, but cleaning my money and holding my stash. That could have got you serious years."

"Jay, there's two types of people in the world: People making money for themselves, and people making money for someone else. You know what type we are?" Mr. Tolliver looks directly in the young man's eyes, and the two grin simultaneously. "Exactly. Congrats on getting out. The plane tickets will be delivered to the address you gave me at noon."

"Perfect."

"Now that we're no longer business partners, and you're just my former student intern, how did you last so long and never get arrested?"

"Cops aren't creative. If you keep your name out of their mouths you're good. I don't live beyond my means. I use transit to make deliveries. Double wrap and vacuum seal my product so no one smells what I'm carrying."

"Yeah, but you have rules…"

"Of course. Number one: only sell in bulk. Number two: always deliver to peoples' homes. Number three: new clients have to be invited by past clients. That's really it. Keep it simple. I could never sell on the streets; too much competition for not enough money. I don't like chemicals, but people who smoke weed, use 'shrooms, just want a personal stash and privacy. I give them that, and they trust that I go out of my way to find the best quality product. Some other stuff, like don't sell to pregnant women. You know, the usual."

"So who's taking over your client list?"

"Some street kids. They're small time, but I got them in contact with my suppliers, they already have places to stash their product. This could be a pay raise for them if they don't screw it up."

"Or whoever they've been getting their stuff from might snitch you out."

"They still on the block. Just a bit less. Hopefully, they'll get completely off. By then I'll be gone."

"So." Mr. T looks up as he finishes off his orange juice. "Did you do something interesting last night, or was it the same as usual – listening to old records in your apartment?"

"My apartment's empty," Jevon replies. "Everything is already shipped off to the spot that I had you help me get. I ended up going to a bar, and sleeping in a stranger's bed."

"You got laid! Wow, that's a small miracle," says Mr. Tolliver with a grin.

Jevon just smiles. "You'd be surprised sir," he says. "Anyway, the stock market opens pretty soon, and I have my final delivery to make before I leave. I'll check with a friend of mine to make sure that no one's out to get me, but you're probably making a mountain out of a mole-hill." Jevon stands up. He's wearing khakis, a black golf shirt, and an army green jacket, clothes that blend in almost anywhere he might go. Now he throws his black satchel over his shoulder and walks towards the door.

"I hope you're right." Mr. Tolliver stands up, follows Jay to the door, where the two shake hands before Jevon leaves to make his last delivery as a drug dealer.

It takes Jevon almost two hours by public transit to get to Great Aunt Sapphire's. Sapphire isn't really his Great

Aunt. Jay comes from a culture where older revered members of his extended family are labeled cousin, or Uncle, or Aunt. Plus, it's a great cover for his frequent visits and satisfies her nosy neighbors.

Jevon met Saph at a pot café. He was there to support a friend who was performing poetry, and she was the cool older lady selling juice behind the counter. When she got too sick to go to her job she called him, not knowing what he did for a living, and asked if he knew anyone who delivered. He laughed, adding her to his list of clients.

Great Aunt Saph lives in a neighborhood that's being gentrified. She bought her bungalow generations ago – raised her kids there until they rebelled, lost a husband there, rented it to a lawyer while she learned herbal medicine on the other side of the world, and returned to it with plans to open a small alternative medicine practice before she was diagnosed with cancer.

Jay fits in the neighborhood more than she does, or her house, surrounded by herbs and weeds that cure things. The small house has a certain presence among the young families trying to look proper and the well-to-do hipsters. Jevon rings the door bell, and a frail white woman with an impressive aura opens the door wide, giving him a hug.

"You came before you left!" she proclaims loud enough for her neighbors to hear. "Come in great nephew, let's have some tea."

Entering the bungalow, filled with trinkets from around the world, Jay lays out the bad news he's bearing.

"Aunt Saph, the last time I was leaving here, one of your neighbors asked me to tell my Great Aunt that they want you to clean up your front yard –"

"I heard them boy. Sit beside me on the sofa, I've already made some tea. This should help with that chest infection you're not telling anyone about."

"How do you –"

"That's what Great Aunts are for," she responds as Jevon sits. She pours her secret blend. "It's a shame, isn't it? If you lived somewhere else you would just be a medicine man. I know you've given herbal advice to some of your clients. News travels fast."

"I just pass on the lessons that you taught me."

"But in this world you're a drug dealer. Me, I'm a crazy cat lady – even though I don't own cats!" She laughs, and her whole face seems to smile. "I guess that's better than a few hundred years ago. You'd be a slave, and I'd be burnt at the stake for being a witch!" As the two laugh Sapphire slaps Javon's lap, leaving her hand lightly gripping his thigh.

"Oh, I almost forgot." Jay pulls out a pound of weed from his satchel. "This should hold you off until you find a new supplier. And these are for fun," he adds, bringing out the last of his mushrooms.

Sapphire leans in and kisses Jevon hard on the lips. Jay kisses her back. Their mouths open, and tongues touch. Nose-to-nose the two grin. "Should you be kissing your great nephew?" Jevon asks, still smiling. "He has a chest infection."

"Can you think of a better way to die than from a young, attractive person's kiss?" she responds. "If I was young, or healthy, or both, I would jump your bones. You've always stopped by and taken care of me when no one else has. For no rational reason."

Jay squeezes the hand on his thigh before finishing his tea and standing up. "Get up so I can give you one last hug."

Sapphire gingerly rises. Jay can smell the faint scent of vanilla and Dove soap. She must have just stepped out of the shower, expecting him to visit. Through her clothing Jevon can feel her small, sagging breasts press against his belly, and he counts her ribs within his embrace. Saph buries her forehead beneath his ribcage. She pulls him as tightly as she can around his hips. The two hold one another for several minutes in silence. He looks downward at her small frame. Watches her upper body shake as she sobs into his chest. When Jay finally releases his grip, he can see tears rolling down her face. Bending over and kissing her again, he squeezes her hands once more, looks deeply into her blue-grey eyes, before seeing himself out the door.

"It must be allergy season," Jay tells himself, wiping tears from his face as he steps away from Sapphire's doorstep.

Jay's plan was to run errands, head to his apartment, and hand his key over before heading to the airport. But since Mr. Tolliver shared his concerns, he's decided to head to his local record store first. The owner knows lots of people – both good and bad – and he'll tell you anything you need to know. All you have to do is be a paying customer, and Jevon has purchased thousands of records there. When he gets to the store, the owner is mumbling fiercely in the back. As Jevon enters, the owner points his ire in his direction.

"Who the hell steals a record and leaves the jacket?" the old man asks. "Now I gotta go through all these cases and make sure I actually got the damn things." Scanning through his merchandise, he spots an original pressing of the soundtrack for *Black Orpheus*. "Jay, you got this?" he asks, lifting the record in his hand.

"Nah," Jevon replies.

"You do now." The old man passes the valuable pressing in its pristine sleeve to Jevon. "While you're here, put it on the turntable and listen to it with me." Jevon slips out the record, walks to the turntable by the cash register, turns it on, fits the vinyl onto it, and places the stylus on the first track.

Sitting down on a stool by the turntable, Jevon listens to the opening guitar riff played gently before the crashing samba beat comes in, accompanied by crowd noise. For nearly forty minutes the record plays samba rhythms, broken up by bossa influenced ballads. The exception, a song that has vocals that sound more African than Brazilian. The drum pattern reminds Jay of a dancehall reggae riddim.

"What's this?" he asks.

"It's probably inspired by voodoo," the shop owner explains.

Jevon's helped out in the past, so as people approach the front counter, he slides behind the register, takes their cash, and gives them a bag before settling back on the stool. He's served three customers by the time the record ends. The old man sighs, gives up on his investigation, and walks towards the counter, where he picks the record off the turntable and returns it to its jacket.

"How much old man?" asks Jevon.

"What does it say on the sticker?"

"Thirty."

"How bout twenty-five?"

"Twenty cash work?"

"Sounds good," the old man replies. Jevon slaps down a twenty, but before he takes his first step towards the door he hears an unusual statement. "Wait a minute, let me write you a receipt." Jevon has been coming here for five years, and has never been given a receipt.

On a small piece of paper, the old man prints in red ink: *Someone's been asking around about you. I told them you split town.*

"Do you know the tale of Orpheus and the Underworld?" asks the old man.

"Yeah."

"It's Greek, or Roman, or something. It's the story of a guy who goes down to hell to save his woman. He goes through these crazy adventures to get down there, save her and get permission to bring her to the world of the living. The god he negotiates with is mad impressed at this kid's bravery so he lets her go, but makes him promise to never look back on his way out of hell. You know what he does?"

"He looks back."

The old man smiles at Jevon, turns towards his shelved inventory, determined to inspect every record in the store.

"Keep bein' old, old man," Jay yells as he steps towards the door.

"As apposed to what?"

"Dead. Don't be dead."

"You and I can agree on that," the storekeeper mumbles before yelling, "I have a name you know!"

"See you Ray!" Jevon calls out. As he gets to the door, he turns back, walks towards the front counter and grabs a plastic bag. Sliding his purchase into it, he eases out the front door while putting a pair of shades on, and begins to walk away at a brisk pace.

His satchel now empty, he slips the plastic bag in, pulls an old pay-as-you-go cell from the back pocket of his khakis, and calls Mr. Tolliver while walking west from the record shop.

"Sir, you were right about the distributor planning something. Don't worry, he doesn't know about you, and I'm leaving town right now."

"Good luck son."

"You too Mr. T."

Breaking it in two, he tosses the cell phone in the trash, grabs his personal phone from his front left pant pocket, and makes another call while dodging cars and pedestrians.

"Hey stranger. Drop everything. We're leaving now –

"Where? You know where. You got the tickets around lunch –

"No, if we look back, I'll lose you."

Jay ends the call, erases the last few numbers on his cell and hands the phone to a homeless man.

"You can sell it, but I'd use it to call a friend. It isn't gonna be disconnected 'til the end of the month."

Before getting a reply, Jevon jumps in a cab and heads to the airport.

# The Failures

The few flaws I have are hidden: masked with blush and liquid makeup. It takes me two hours on a good day to hide my blemishes – chase the scars away. My outfit is always the perfect combination of H&M, Old Navy, GAP, and Urban Outfitter. Shoes? Something I found at a boutique for a day's wages. I look how I feel – perfect. Oh damn, there's a run in my stockings. Okay, almost perfect. After I change these stockings I'll look perfect.

I have my own condo, a boyfriend far enough away that I can secretly have multiple lovers and a good paying job – that I hate. I should have gone into marketing instead of human resources at business school. I'm constantly surrounded by losers who can't keep jobs at the employment agency. Don't they get it? If you're a loser accept your place in life. Why must I be the one to tell people what jobs they're qualified for? Why don't they get it? Anyway, as soon as I change these stockings I better get out of here, or I'll be late.

Public transit is a necessary evil downtown. My car is a weekday afterthought except for the times I go out to bars or concerts. Being close to so many people is a gamble. You never know if the person beside you bathed. If a seat is open, I still make sure not to sit beside certain men – no one wants to look easy. More importantly, black men are scary – that's what makes them such a wonderful sexual fetish.

Today, I get to work early. In the break room, Amy is making coffee.

"Hi Amy, what a nice dress," if you're into wearing granny hand me downs. "Where did you find it?"

"My husband and I drove to an amazing auction in the countryside last weekend. We found some great antique furniture, he found some books for his collection, and I found this." Why is this woman modelling her find for me? It's like parading death. "This is the real deal. It's Coco Chanel. I probably shouldn't wear it. I should just put it in a glass case, but I thought, let me wear it once." Now she's showing off. Showing off the clothes of a dead person, designed by a dead person. Wonderful.

I smile, mumble an impressed reaction, pour my first mug of coffee, and head to my desk to check emails. Not for the first time I'm employee of the month – I've successfully found jobs for eighty people. We all hire hundreds of people a month, but most of them are fodder to hit goals. Getting eighty to stick in a role and get past training is big. That's an additional check from our client, over and above the cut we get from their wages.

"Okay people!" Our manager Shawn is one of those Anthony Robbins positive reinforcement guys. "Great job this month! I've emailed you all roles that I want you to get filled. Go through the database of resumés and book those interviews!" With that, the doors for the agency open.

This is the most depressing part of the day. These miserable, desperate men and women of all races and ages trudge into our offices in their Sunday best. Some see us as saviours – those are the ones who smile, seem straightforward, and look at you without fear. Most are here out of desperation – they are broken. The pride that made them think that they could find employment on their own has been crushed. They look at the floor, afraid to see their fate in a fellow client's eyes. To me they're all losers. My job is to merely figure out which ones I can help, and which ones I can pass off to another agent. That's why I have such a high success rate.

Today starts with a cute Hispanic boy with limited work experience. He has more chance of finding his way into my bed than finding a job. But he's here, might as well let him go through the process. "Hi Jorge, my name is Becca." My name's actually Amy but everyone here uses pseudonyms. "Before we talk, I'm going to take you to a computer station to test your knowledge of office software and your typing skills. This should only take about half an hour. Please follow me."

I stand up, straighten myself, and lead him with my swaying hips to the computer station. After setting the tests required for the roles that I think Jorge might qualify for, I tell him, "When you're done, the computer will let me know, so stay here and I'll come and get you." Walking away, I can feel him watching me.

As I reach my desk I can hear Shawn flirting with a female candidate, the gossipers in the break room, an interview with a frustrated black man — is there any other type? I quietly call a client who we failed to help last month. "Hello, can I speak to your editor please? Hi this is Becca from ABC Employment. Yes, I told you that we primarily looked at candidates for call centre and clerical roles last month, but it looks like we might have found a candidate for your junior editor role. He doesn't have the required experience, but I think I can convince him to take on the role as an internship. Yes, you'd still have to pay our fees but think of the savings you'll have not paying him for three months. Okay, I'm sending you his resumé now, goodbye." Now all I have to do is fool this kid into working for free.

His test results are back — wow these are better than I thought. Time to get him. After chatting with Beth to plan lunch, I grab Jorge and lead him back to my desk.

"Well, after looking over your resumé and checking your test results I think you would be perfect for a customer service call centre. You speak multiple languages, you're well educated. The only issue with your preferred industry is that you lack experience. Why is it that you have such a big gap in your resumé?"

"My grandparents are from Latin America, but I had never been down there. When I graduated from journalism school I was offered an opportunity to work as a correspondent for a South American magazine. I couldn't say no. Unfortunately, when I got back home none of the local media wanted to recognize my experience. The only exception was in the local Latino community, but the job offers I got —"

"Here's the thing Jorge, can I call you Jorge? You're still really young. What you should do now is intern somewhere for three to six months." Then in a lowered voice I continue. "We're not supposed to do this, but I have a friend who might have an internship opportunity in publishing. Would you be interested?"

After a brief pause he agrees. "Sure, but I need something to tie me over financially as well."

I got him. "No problem, I'll pass your resumé on to my friend for the publishing internship and forward it to the bilingual call centre job that I just mentioned as well. Sound good?" Big smile on my face. He responds in kind.

"Sounds good," he agrees, and just like that I have

double the commission for a single interview. I give him my card, and because I've framed it like the internship is an act of kindness, I feel comfortable telling him to call me to let me know how it goes, and suggest that we could talk about the internship over coffee – since it's not the agency's business.

I check my watch, realize that I haven't had my second coffee, and head to the break room. There I find Beth.

"Hey Becca, how was your first interview today? Same evil schemes to convince slops into long-term jobs that they don't want?"

"Even better, I just got a boy to take a call centre job, and a free internship that I'm getting commission on and he doesn't realize it. And it's my diversity hire for the day. I didn't even have to get a job for one of those know-it-all black ladies. Plus, by next week that boy will be in my bed. This is too easy."

"You're kind of evil Becca – that's why I love you." Beth's grin slowly envelopes her face as she laughs. I steal an apple from the fridge, finish it, and head to my desk before looking at my numbers – I'm only one more customer service hire from hitting my quota for the month. I want to be conquered, and I know the big, black, unemployed man for the job.

He is so scary that I get excited thinking about him. If I hit quota by lunch I'm leaving work early to be his slave.

As I calm down from my carnal excitement, my next

potential hire approaches my desk. With such a bare resumé I assumed that he would be much younger. With older candidates I speak to them first: it might not be worth my time having them do computer tests. They might not even know how to use computers.

"Please sit down mister –"

"Reginald, please just call me Reginald." He even has an old person name.

"Reginald, how can ABC Employment assist you today?"

"I realize my resumé is sort of barren, and I'm not the youngest person in the room, but I was hoping that you guys could help me find something. Even a part-time job would work for me."

"Do you have any computer skills at all?" I enquire with my fictional genuine smile.

"Of course. My church has job skill training. I'm there every week." Good, I might be able to leave work early.

"Are you looking for anything in particular?"

"Oh no, you're the expert. I'll leave my trust in you –"

"Becca, my name is Becca." I inform him while pointing at the placard on my desk. "So why so little job experience?"

"For over twenty years I was a professional dancer. Ballet mainly, but some modern. I toured the world, and danced with some wonderful companies. Sadly my feet failed me – like most dancers. I broke too many bones, too many times. I tried becoming a choreographer but there were always younger, more innovative, more politically skilled choreographers."

"And nothing after that?" I pry further.

"No, somewhere along the way I met the most extraordinary man," oh he's gay. "He was one of those corporate patrons of the arts. I don't know if it was a marriage or a corporate sponsorship." Reginald's laughter suddenly fills the office space. Murmurs dim, vacant faces turn in our direction out of curiosity.

"Sadly, my husband left this world last year." It was probably AIDS. Should I ask Reginald about his health? Is he healthy enough to work? "The relatives who all disowned him suddenly came out of the woodwork. I fought them, won, but found that I need a job to offset my budget. Either that, or sell his place and move somewhere smaller. I want to keep his place as long as I can. It reminds me of the blessed grinch."

"Sorry for asking, but is it okay if I ask how he died?" Legally I'm not allowed to ask, but I'm sure Shawn will understand my situation if the candidate gets upset.

"Why are you so formal love? He had a heart attack. The old fart didn't listen to me when I told him that old people are supposed to retire from high stress jobs." That was easier than I thought.

"So you were a world class dancer, who retired and married a millionaire," and now you've fallen so far that you're here? "That sounds magical."

"That wasn't the magic." Reginald calmly straightens

his blazer. "The magic was finally finding love so late in life. Love is such an amazing thing."

"Yes, yes it is." I nod, but I have no clue what he's talking about. To me, having a life empty of emotional investment is much better. I don't want to be this man. I wouldn't wish the pain he's experienced losing his husband on my worst enemy. My way is better – there is no pain.

I stand up and guide Reginald to the computer testing centre. When I get to my desk I start texting mister Right Now. He's free, tells me to book the same hotel for this afternoon, and to send him a text with the number of the room when I get there. Without hesitation, I book the room online. Maybe I should buy new lingerie on the way there. Will he like what I'm wearing right now? Do I care? Yes, the last thing I want breaking my perfection is shoddy underwear. So easily remedied as well – silly me.

When I look up, one of the other agents, feeling sorry for the old man in the computer testing centre, has walked Reginald back to my desk. I check his results, and he wasn't lying, he does have passable computer skills. I offer him the final customer service call centre job that I need to fill for my quota and he accepts it. As Reginald walks away I think… What a loser! He's a man who ran his own freelance career, who probably has some corporate connections thanks to his late husband; if he pressured me, I probably would have had to pitch his resumé to a couple businesses for managerial positions. But what do I care? My quota is filled. He should know better. He should understand how to shape his resumé. What a loser.

Pushing away from my desk, I make a call out to Beth. She's finishing off an interview. Five minutes later, we're out the door searching for a deal for lunch. Usually we're arguing over the best sushi special, but with my planned sexual escapade for this afternoon I convince Beth to follow me to a salad bar. It's easy to swing her eating habits – she's not exactly slim. I feel guilty, but I can't have my breath ruining this tryst.

At our food court table, I share my plans for the afternoon. Beth lives vicariously through me. She does have boyfriends that she flirts with. Men that she shares emails and pictures with, but she's too afraid to lose her kids, and her comfortable love life with the husband.

I've seen her flirt with some incredible big, dark, men. I often wonder what would happen if I locked her in a room with a virile, young, naked black man. She probably would throw it all away for a night. It's likely that knowledge that keeps her from dipping her toe in the deep end. I'm so lucky to not have that sort of responsibility.

After lunch, we head to a lingerie shop. Beth wanted some new bras, but I convince her to buy a corset. She claims it's over her budget, but I'm sure her husband will not complain. He'll probably thank me.

Not to be outdone, I go all out buying garter belts, knee-high stockings, a sheer thong and a matching bra. I look damn good. More importantly, I feel damn good. We happily carry our items in unmarked shopping bags, slide behind our desks and giggle in each other's direction as Shawn makes his afternoon rounds.

Shawn is a bit edgy. Apparently, someone ate one of his homegrown organic apples. I didn't realize that it was a special apple. It just looked a bit smaller to me. But this fool is asking everyone about the apple. I look down and see the core in my trash bin. I pick it up, wrap it in a tissue and put it in my pocket. I've hit my quota for the month, and I've done most of my interviews for the day. I quickly ask Beth to take the candidates I had planned to interview this afternoon. She takes them, confident in my ability to filter through resumés. To her, it's free money that I'm offering.

"Shawn my stomach is upset." Before he can ask for details I slip out.

On the street I dump the apple in a public trash can and head to the hotel. I text him to come early, but he's busy. After a drink at the hotel bar, I head upstairs, order a bottle of wine, draw a bath and sink into the tub. I get out after half an hour and change into my lingerie. My phone rings, it's a text from him. He's going to be late. I order more bottles of wine, and turn on the hotel pay-per-view to whet my appetite. Posing in front of the mirror, I spend half of the porn admiring myself.

Maybe I should call my boyfriend to fill the time. That's weird. There's no answer.

It would be cool to drop everything and travel like Jorge. Have a family to care for like Beth. Be dedicated to your job like Shawn. Find the love of your life after having a career like Reginald. Even Amy and her husband scouring rural thrift shops to fill their weird house with bad kitsch items has its pluses. They all have something personal to hold on to. Something they give a damn about that makes them human. But all I have is this perfect body, sense of style, and beauty. It's all skin deep. Speaking of skin, I'm a woman who gets off having sex with men who scare me, in my day-to-day existence, because of their skin. When he finally comes, I will beg him to fill the void that this existence creates with terror and masculinity. I will grovel on my knees. I shall submit.

Three-quarters through the movie and someone finally answers my boyfriend's phone. I know that it's work hours, but this is ridiculous. I draw a breath, ready to berate him, but before I say anything I hear a female voice. As I hang up, there's a knock on the door. Reapplying my makeup, I turn off the TV, open the door and greet him.

"Hi daddy. I've been waiting all day for you."

## The Long Way Home

Every day I wake up at 6 AM. It's always the exact same ritual: first the socks, then boxer-briefs, a long sleeve compression shirt, shorts, and my favourite runners. After getting clothed, I grab an apple and I'm out the door. On cold days I wear spandex tights under my shorts. They look stupid but they keep me pretty warm. By quarter to seven I'm on the usual path in the park near my apartment.

When I started running here, I didn't even know about this trail. To be honest, I got lost, but my sense of direction told me it was headed towards my place. I hate running through it because it's not paved, and I end up spending hours a week cleaning mud off my shoes and running clothes. But that first time I ran through this trail we crossed paths.

Now it's a daily ritual. I run through this isolated part of my local park. Only two of us ever seem to run this route. For some reason I feel compelled to cross her path. I think that it's less an attraction than a curiosity that drives me. Witnessing life crumbling must be a fascination of mine. Or maybe I find her strangely attractive and am in denial. I can't explain the rationality of my feelings. Always at ten minutes past seven we cross paths beside the north end of the pond. Every day I see her, she has shrunken into herself again.

So slim. A figurine built of skin and bone – little else remains. All that made her feminine no longer present. The only thing left is the shell of someone. But each time, she smiles that same smile. It's the only genuine face that I witness all day. A load is lifted. Seeing that smile is my addiction.

However, these past months I've been the only jogger on our trail. Rain, sunshine or snow, that mirage of a woman that could be blown away by a soft gust appeared in front of my eyes. Here I am. Still running this stupid, muddy trail. Maybe the interest was one way. Maybe she found a trail with less mud and more isolated. Maybe she died from whatever was making her so skinny. She couldn't have been eating much.

You know, a part of me was repulsed by her. "How could anyone not realize that they are killing themselves? Why didn't she stop?" But another side wished I could follow her compulsion – stop eating or drinking liquids for weeks at a time. Take before and after photos to document my fall from grace. Attempt to understand the pleasure of withholding necessity; the pain that drives such personal cruelty. How did my gaze feel? Did you think that I looked at you like I felt sorry for you? Condescending? Did you feel objectified? Was the curiosity mutual, or did you think I was a stalker?

What's that sound? Oh, my alarm clock. I've got to get ready for my jog. This feels like Groundhog Day, except I missed my chance to alter my fate. There's no time to hit the snooze bar. Against my better instincts, I roll out of bed. Head to the washroom and use the toilet. Wash my face. Brush my teeth. There's no sense in having a shower before my run. It's always the same ritual. My running clothes are on the top of my dresser. I disrobe. Grab and put on my socks, then my boxer-briefs, an old compression shirt, today is supposed to be cold so I pull on spandex tights, my shorts and then my favourite runners. A fresh apple is waiting for me on my kitchen counter. I grab it. Rub it clean against my shirt and take a bite as I lock my apartment and head out for my jog. These sneakers are brand new. Why am I still running this stupid trail?

Waking up at 5 AM, I have my shower, do my hair and makeup, change into the newest spandex leggings and matching sports bra, drink a glass of water and run out the door. My health is better than it has been in the past. I used to be so embarrassed when I went running. I knew how skinny I was. I was literally skin and bones. I knew I was killing myself – it was compulsion.

People don't get it. I saw those looks. Those shocked, disappointing eyes that say, "Gross, how could you do that to yourself?" But I still wanted to run. First I started jogging earlier and earlier. But there were still people staring at me. One day I found a quiet path, a dirt trail everyone avoided. Finally, I had a peaceful space, away from those disappointed, horrified glares.

That was my trail. I had it to myself. When life had me down, it was my secret garden. But one day, on my early morning run, he appeared. First, I was surprised. Then, I felt fear. Why was he here? This my secret trail. Don't look at me with those pitiful eyes. As we neared one another, I found him surprisingly attractive. If he gave me those... Will I lose my sanctuary?

We crossed paths. I shyly smiled. His eyes were so calming. I felt empowered. He was different than everyone else. For the next six months or so he continued to appear. Appear and look at me without condescension. And at each glance, at each step we took towards one another, at each footprint we created running away from one another, I got stronger.

I called my mom. For the first time in years. I told what happened when I was young. Why I stopped calling her. How I was killing myself. I asked my mom for help. She said yes.

I stopped appearing in front of him. For months I didn't see our trail. Would he still be there when I returned? Those calming eyes that helped me fall asleep at the clinic haunted me. It was his smile that got me through the therapy sessions, the meals, the 24 hour supervision. Now I'm back. My A cup sports bra doesn't flutter. I have a ways to go, but I almost look beautiful. I have this compulsion still, but it's pretty much dormant. I want to show that mysterious, gracious soul who I've become.

My first jog as a free woman. Free from the chains that pulled me into an eating disorder. Free from the doctors and nurses. Free from those – from those eyes.

After jogging down the sidewalk for three blocks, I reach the park. I've been running for two minutes on one of the smaller paved walks. Finally, I see the entrance to the trail – our trail. My pace quickens slightly as I enter the muddy, rocky path. My face fails to hide my excitement. I can sense he's there. It feels like fate.

At the same place we always cross paths, I see him. He hasn't quit running this route. I slow down to a walking pace. As he gets closer, he stops running too. Here he is walking towards me. This wasn't one-sided. This is fate. Almost arm's length in front of one another we stop walking.

"I haven't seen you for a while."

These are the first words that we've ever shared. They're accompanied by that same gorgeous smile.

"Well, I'm back." This smile is big. My face is hurting. "I've been gone for a while. I didn't know if you were still going to be here."

He scans me up and down. I swear it must take everything in his power to not lick his lips.

This bastard can't even hide his motives. He went out of his way to see me, all of this time, for sex.

"Of course I still run this way. I don't mind the mud, and it's beautiful, and quiet."

– Yeah right.

"Well, you're looking really good. I see you've been taking care of yourself."

Fuck. Why are men like this? Why am I still in front of him? I can give a polite goodbye, and change my schedule tomorrow. I don't have to let him see me. Why am I still fucking smiling? Do I like this? Am I this desperate for attention? He's going to ask for my number isn't he? Why else would he have his phone with him? I'm about to give him my actual number. I can't believe that I'm doing this. What the fuck is wrong with me?

# Rastavarius

"Djembe players who participate in voodoo ritual often leave alcoholic spirits near the open-mouth of their resting drums. They symbolically give the spirit of the instrument an offering. Maybe that's what you have to do with your violin. Give it something; symbolic, or real. Let it know that it is your beloved partner." That's Rastaman. We're in a complex of practice studios. I've been struggling with Rózsa's Violin Concerto. The door of the studio that I'm subletting was open. Rastaman heard me complaining to myself and invited me here.

We're surrounded by tealight candles and incense. On the floor is an Indian rug. Rastaman is one of the few musicians who lives where he practices. For some reason, we hit it off when I started coming here. Now, the band space that I rented to get away from the classical community has turned into three hour practices with intermittent dreadlock Rastafarian therapy.

"So what you're saying is that I should worship my violin?" I don't even bother to hide my disbelief.

"No dread, you're missing the point." I can barely see Rastaman sitting on the sofa across the studio from me, drinking loose leaf tea. "You have all the talent in the world. The difference between you and a great musician is your relationship with your instrument. To you, it's just a piece of wood to manipulate. The djembe player can drive worshippers into ecstatic states simply because they consider the inanimate object they play a part of themselves."

"Violin isn't the same," I counter. "There are only so many great violins. They are usually owned by wealthy people who loan them out to the most talented, respected players." After sipping at my tea I continue, "Those violins are alive. The piece of work that I have, I don't know. It might be a newborn child, or it might be a doll."

"The only thing that makes a Stradivarius more prestigious to a normal person, is the prestige of the person playing it, dread. Treat your instrument like a child and it shall show you its love."

"Thanks for the tea Rastaman." Placing my teacup on a saucer on the rug, I stand up and leave his space.

"No problem dread. You'll figure things."

I nod without turning my head to acknowledge his words and head to my room.

I've been subletting from a band that's been on tour for two months. They come back in two weeks, around the time that my competition starts. Until then, this barren room is my personal prison. Twice a day for three hours I practice. White walls, leather sofa, and a small boombox are all that I see for six hours a day; seven days a week.

Violins are mysterious instruments. For your first year, year and a half, you sound like a screechy death match between a cat and a pigeon. Then one day you sound like you can play a violin. From there it's a race to perfection. First you master a myriad of songs, arpeggios and scales in the first position – the lowest range on the fingerboard. Then you're introduced to the third position – your first finger lands where your third finger would in first position. By the time you're playing songs that feature fifth position sequences you're comfortable playing high notes with clarity.

No one knows who will reach near-perfection first. Will it be the phenom virtuoso who achieves an elite level before their teens? The inner-city kid who is discovered making a $50 violin sound like an $800 violin? Or the kid who slowly progresses, looks up one day, and realizes that they are touring the world.

There is no simple path. For me this small competition is an important step. For others, it's probably a warmup to a bigger competition in Europe or Asia. I've already prepared my mandatory preliminary piece. For the second round, I'll be using an old favourite. But the choices for the final round – a selection of works featuring orchestral accompaniment – were limited. If I want to win, I'll have to play a piece that I figure other violinists will avoid, considering the lack of time to perfect it. We just got the options for the final round last week. To me, it was obvious that my only choice was the Rózsa concerto.

It has everything: moving chords (playing multiple strings at the same time while fingering changes), harmonic notes (when you lightly press down on the string and the vibration between your finger and the string creates a note octaves higher than the note would be if the finger was pressed down properly), incredibly fast passages, and full use of the fingerboard.

Rózsa was the Hungarian composer who created the score for Ben-Hur. After perfecting this work with collaborator Jascha Heifetz – the violinist he composed it for – he adapted portions for the film "The Private Life of Sherlock Holmes." That means not only is this work difficult, but every judge and some members of the audience will know it by heart. I have no time to worry. I hit play on the boombox and attempt to play along with the recording.

After three failed run-throughs, I'm forced to practice passages without support. After two hours of drilling the fingering and transitions between positions into my head, I successfully get through the piece once – at a much slower speed than the recording. I pack my violin into its case and get ready to leave.

With my violin case on my back I head to Rastaman's practice studio/living space. The door's open. His band is playing some Jimmy Cliff. I lean against the frame of the door and listen:

> And this loneliness won't leave me alone
> It's such a drag to be on your own
> My woman left me and she didn't say why
> Well I guess, I have to try
> Many rivers to cross...

As they finish, Rastaman looks up at me and shouts out, "Dread, don't forget our conversation! Trust me, I know instruments – you can call me Rastavarius."

Smiling at his joke, I nod and wave, take a step into the now dark hallway, and disappear into the night on my way home.

I live in a series of low income lofts that have been taken over by musicians and visual artists. Under normal circumstances it's the ideal place to practice – my usual piano accompanist lives a few doors down. Unfortunately, I'm not the only person who lives here that's in this competition. When one of my neighbours told me about the band space being available I jumped at it.

When I get inside my apartment, I notice that someone's broken in – again. This time it's Alexa, a painter who just moved in across the hallway. She's asleep on my sofa, watching one of my old Kurosawa DVDs. After I jerry-rig the latch again, I wrap a blanket around her, shut off the TV and turn on the radio.

I'm listening to a fascinating audio documentary on a group of rural DJs and eating a bowl of frosted shredded wheat when she decides to wake up. "What happened?"

"The good guys won. It's generally the journey that matters in these samurai movies, not the destination," I explain, while slurping back the almond milk left in the bowl.

"Why don't you have anything good to eat in here?" she asks. Not even bothering to apologize for breaking into my apartment.

"Why don't you have anything to eat at your place?" I reply, tongue placed firmly in cheek.

"Because I'm a struggling artist —"

"It's like you already knew the answer." My sarcastic tone makes her sit up and look at me.

"What makes a black man think he can become a violinist and not make hip-hop music?"

That's a low blow.

"Nothing wrong with bands like Black Violin and Nuttin' But Stringz. I respect the hell out of those kids. They're making the violin cool. There used to be jazz violin players back in the day as well. It's fun, but it's not me. I like the challenge of perfecting a work that can sometimes have ties to a tradition hundreds of years old."

"Cool. How was your day?" Alexa gets up and opens my bare fridge, pours herself a glass of my orange juice and comes back to the sofa. This is when I notice that she's in her pyjamas.

"I had a conversation with Rastaman about my problems with the concerto –"

"You mean THE Rastaman? Who used to tour the world, and was signed to one of the big reggae labels in the nineties?" she asks, cutting me off.

"Yeah," I reply. "Money's tight and he's between tours, so he's living in a session studio in the same building that I'm subletting a room. Anyway, when I was talking about my struggles with this piece he told me about how voodoo drummers give offerings to their instruments. Sounds weird doesn't it?" When I look up, I can see the gleam in her eyes, and the excitement on her face.

"We should do it," she declares.

"Do what? It? Like have sex?" I know what she's saying, but I'm trying to deflect.

"No, make an offering to your violin. It'll be fun!"

Before I can respond, Alexa is out the door. When she returns her arms are full with tealight candles, essential oils, sticks of incense and various holders. She can barely carry everything. I rush towards her and grab a few items. Briefly, I can feel her breath on my neck. We smile at each other and head to the centre of my room.

Alexa makes a large circle with the candles. Inside the circle, she creates a square, using incense sticks and essential oil lamps. She asks me to light everything. We find a blanket among my things, fold it to add thickness, and place it in the centre of the circle. We then set the violin on the blanket. Finally, I pour the last of my rum in a glass and place it at the head of the violin. The two of us sit on the floor on opposite sides of the instrument, hold hands to make a circle, and close our eyes.

"How long do we have to do this?" I whisper.

"Sh. Just concentrate on your violin. How you got it, how it looks, all the nuances of it, and how it sounds."

I remember exactly how I got this violin. My parents knew that I had two choices: get a new violin, or quit playing. I had outgrown the one that I had. My violin teacher was astonished that I could pull such a powerful sound out of such a pathetic instrument and was frustrated. She swore that I was falling behind other violinists my age who had better instruments. By fluke, my dad came across one at an estate sale. He wasn't confident that it was any good, but it was only $50. When my teacher had a look at it she was pleased – it turned out to be a handmade American fiddle from the 1920's. More importantly, the rich tone fit my playing style.

I remember the first time I played it after changing the strings, replacing the fingerboard and buying a new bridge. How powerful slow melodic pieces sounded on it. I think about the small scratches that I tried to polish out of it. All the work that I personally put into the instrument.

Half an hour later, I open my eyes. Alexa's are already open. Holding hands we stand up and walk outside the circle before speaking. "What do we do now?" I ask.

"Leave everything until the candles burn out," she replies. "Can I sleep here?"

Now I know the real reason she came to my apartment. "Sure, but no sex," I answer with a grin.

"Why haven't we had sex yet?" she jokes, reflecting my grin back at me.

"I don't know how many lofts you've broken into."

"All of them. But everyone else gets angry. Plus, I don't feel safe accidentally falling asleep in their rooms."

"You would feel a lot safer in mine if you fixed the lock after you broke in, and lock the door behind yourself," I suggest while giving her cut-eye. Alexa doesn't care. She's wrapped in a blanket on my futon underneath the big window, and I'm still standing. I grab something to sleep in, have a quick shower, brush my teeth and jump into bed with the cat burglar. After a few minutes of wrestling over the blankets, we settle in. I find myself spooning her small frame as I drift into a slumber.

The next day I wake up to the smell of pancakes and bacon. Alexa explains to me how much easier it was to get food from the other neighbours if she mentioned my name. One person gave her eggs for the pancakes and another gave her bacon in exchange for a debt that he had with me. I smile, try to pretend that she's not wearing one of my shirts, and look down to see my violin still on the floor. Lying there, surrounded by burnt out candles and incense.

I pack my violin in its case. Drink the rum from the glass on the floor. Change into clean clothes, unashamed that Alexa keeps stealing looks at me naked. Rolling a couple pieces of bacon into a pancake, I gobble it down, before drinking a glass of tap water and leaving.

Before heading to my part-time job I have a short session with my current teacher. We spend half of the hour quickly running through the first two pieces. The second half we talk about options if I can't get the Rózsa. She notices a small improvement in my playing, but I don't. Afterwards, I head to my job at the classical music store selling sheet music.

When I arrive at the practice studio Rastaman is clearing out. He's directing movers and his band while leaning on a wall. "Be gentle with that box breda. It has mi favourite tea set," Rastaman explains to a burly man who nods in his direction. "Dread," Rastaman calls out to me. "I'm glad to see you before I leave. My first world tour in ten years, can you believe it? How's the violin?"

"My teacher notices improvement, but I can't yet."

Rastaman walks up to me, looks me straight in the eye and says, "Tch, you did the ritual didn't you? Trust me, your teacher can hear it. Soon you will too." He gives me a hug, nods his head, and waves in my direction while walking away.

After sitting in my practice studio for fifteen minutes,

I unpack my violin. Hit play on the boombox, and for the first time, I finally get through the concerto at proper tempo. It was sloppier than hell, but it's a start. With less than two weeks left, I've turned a corner.

Five days later Alexa stopped breaking into other peoples' apartments. Two days after that she moved in with me, not seeing the point in paying full rent if she could pay half. Two days before the competition I gave her my second key. The next day we went shopping for a black suit. It wasn't until I stood on stage during the preliminaries that I absorbed how much better a violinist I had become. It wasn't until the final day that I fully grasped the importance of understanding the idiosyncrasies of an instrument.

Before going on stage, I admire the suit that Alexa picked. Look down at my violin and smile. The conductor touches my shoulder to let me know it's our time. I tuck my violin beneath my arm and we stroll out to a polite applause – I can hear Alexa's cheers. As the audience falls into silence, the violin rests beneath my chin. I can hear the timpani and bassoon, then the clarinet. I raise my bow and begin.

## The Benefit of Friendship

Long time we tell me self, "Don't mess wit' light-skin gal." When Norm finally graduate and move back home, Jaz move in. Me pay no mind. Dat likkle white April friend; 2 likkle gal arm in arm. Talk bout dem "besties," for long time. Me can respec' dat.

Me notice likkle ting bout Jazmine. She light-skinned, born here, live 50 mile from here her whole life, but nuff man ask her, "Where are you from?" As if she foreign. Quietly, mi find dat hilarious. I dread rasta workin on post grad degree, but she de foreigner. Lawd.

Maybe 2-3 months, she watch TV, me sit down watch. No words. Housemates want potluck, she ask fi salt, I pass it. No words. Wasn't til April brudda, mi bredren who got me a room in dis house, Jacob pass through. Him want to visit him likkle sis, but sistren gone work.

Jake ask me to go bar, but before we leave, him knock on Jazmine door.

When I see inside, me flip out on de likkle gal. Hippy gal dat. Witch wit no sense dat. No furniture, just lava lamp and clothes and ting in campin' bags. Dem glow in dark star sticker all ova de wall and ceilin'. Air mattress and sleepin' bag fi sleep. What a travesty dat!

Next day, Jacob get van from work, I take time off from studies and the three a we go furniture huntin'. First, down lane where nuff furniture get dumped pon sidewalk. Second, Salvation Army. Third, thrift shops. Since I complain, I spend money. Jaz still cheap. Pick weirdest pieces – me swear. I get her a new mattress from ghetto furniture store me know. Dat hippy wanted to grab thrown out mattress. Bed bug hotel dat.

I spend more on mattress than anyting else. Cheap gal dat. After Jake and me carry furniture to her room and leave her to make ting proper, me assume ting go back to normal. Me don't mess wit light-skin gal. Me grad student, we have no time fi hippy gal like dat.

2 week later, Jake and Jaz start dating. Cool. Me wonda how man know gal so long, since she his sister's "bestie," and dem just hook up. But we keep tings to me self.

Slowly tings change. Me hear Jaz's story. She start job soon as she graduate high school, but parents try sabotage her. Steal from her. Took gal 2 years to move out. She would go campin' to escape dem. So all she had was campin' equipment. Sein. She and I start talk regular. If Jaz have day off at de store and I break from research we both would watch TV. Sometimes we'd wake up spoonin' on a couch wit TV on. Jake cool, him didn't mind. Plus, him know me na mess wit' light-skinned gal.

Hangin' wit Jaz, me smoke de best weed me have in me life. Dis a 420 house. Nuff weed. But she had de best. Jake, Jaz and I would gather in Jaz room, lock de door, puff, puff, pass and look at sticker on wall. Dat was de crew – Jake, Jaz and Solomon. Everybody in the house thought sex ting. Even April ask we. I answer, "Trust me April, your brother too respectful for that. They hold hand, kiss. That's that."

Dem must a been together 6, 7 months when Jake meet him wife. She Chinese. Me swear, dem together 3 month and him jump on plane wit her to Hong Kong. Dem send me picture of dem and dem kid pon social media on de regular.

Jaz take it in stride. Big respec fi dat. April, her, a bunch a dem likkle gal dem go party a few time. She mess wit' a few man dem, but soon, back to bein' me sistren. Me stay pon sideline fi dat. I in middle of writing Master's dissertation. Had no time anyway.

Dat bring I to today. I bad Doctorate student, part-time teachers' assistant, adjunct professor. Jaz still work at same boutique. I spread eagle, naked pon mattress I buy years ago in her room. Me dreads all ova de place. Five foot Jaz at head of bed sittin' cross-legged over me right shoulder, naked, puffin' on big green glass bong.

Full condom pon de side of waste basket, cause we can't be bothered. What a dis? What me done?

Outside room, big party dat. What we celebrate? Birthday? New job? Long weekend? No, dis first time in time all a we get weekend off at same time. No one work bar, store, call centre, on tour, hustlin'. All housemates, all girlfriend, all boyfriend at party. Except the 2 a we.

I just break rule. More important, have I mashed up friendship for punani? I look up, over me right shoulder. Generally, I prefer 'oman wit' slightly smaller breasts, but she mad sexy – for light-skinned gal, at least.

Mildly disappointed in me self, I let go of sigh. Jaz takes a toke, touches me forehead wit her left hand, looks down a we, and responds back.

"What?"

"What we tell dem?"

"That I had a really good stash of weed. We had some, and fell asleep."

"Dey're not going to believe dat."

"They already think that we're having sex."

"Since when?" I ask, wit a curious look pon we face.

"First, back when we would fall asleep on the couch watching TV together – it took months to explain that. Then, when you Jake and I would smoke in here, they all thought we were having threesomes. The shit they said back then!

"Oh also, remember when we had that week when we held hands everywhere? People read that wrong too.

But after Jake left, and I started to slip into bed with you, because I couldn't sleep, I stopped telling people that we weren't sleeping together. I mean, we didn't have sex, but technically, I was sleeping with you." As Jaz chat 'bout each situation, dat smile on her grow.

"If every 'oman I hold hand wit' I sex up, I would be a bad man," I mutter up to Jaz.

Jaz smiles her biggest smile back down a we. Takes a couple hits from her bong and offers Jah's sacrament. "I can't smoke all of this, you want some?"

I sit up, pull me self to de head of de bed beside Jazmine. Jaz pass I de bong and her lighter. She watches I blow smoke clouds inna air. She straightens her legs. Almost on cue, I pass back de bong, slide back down, place me head pon her lap. Jaz starts to stroke me locks.

"So what dis mean?" I ask.

"What does what mean?" Jazmine asks back.

"This. Now we sleep wit one another, what a dis?" I ask a second time.

"What were we before?"

"Close friends."

"Are we still close friends?"

"Yeah mon," I confirm.

"There's no need to put labels on things."

"Labels important. If me introduce you, what I say? Girlfriend? Matey?"

"I'm not your girlfriend. We've never gone on dates. We hang out. You open doors for me sometimes, but we're not like that. It's always been chill. This is just a natural progression of things, isn't it?" she explains to we. "Why does there have to be a label on this?"

"Me sex friend?" I joke.

"We don't have to fuck ever again. I'm cool with how things were before." Jaz na find me joke funny.

"How 'bout friend with benefits?" I ask slightly more serious. Me hear dis before but not quite overstand it.

"I never understood that one. Isn't the benefit of friendship, friendship?" Jazmine respond back a we, placing de bong beside de lava lamp on her bed stand. Jaz shuts off lamp. Slides down de bed. Reaches for her blankets and covers both a we before lying down beside I. Her head rests on me chest. Her right leg entwine wit me right. I can feel her heart beat pon me right arm.

Fi a quick second we look up. Me swear dat real star. Hemp cookie me take early and weed must kick in same time. Me also noticed silence outside room. How party done so soon?

"Hey Jaz —"

"Yeah?"

"Why's it so quiet?"

"Wha —"

"Isn't dere a party?"

"We went camping. It's just us."

Slowly I sit up. We both naked in Jaz's old sleeping bag. Pon de right, a camp fire. Behind we, our tent. OUR tent. Stars and nature surround we. I look down at Jaz, naked in de sleeping bag.

"What, you don't know how you got here?" Jaz say sarcastic to we without eyes open. "Me don't mess wit' light-skinned gal? Or whatever bullshit you used to say?"

I take a deep breath. Lay back down. Zip up de sleeping bag and kiss pon her forehead. Jazmine smile dat big smile of hers. Me don't care what type a spell dis. Me good.

# A Brief Guide to Gaslighting

I.

-- Gaslighting?

-- Yeah, gaslighting.

-- You make it sound like I'm a narcissist, a sociopath, or some kind of psychopath. I ain't that bad. So what do you want to know?

-- How many?

-- How many people I messed with?

-- Yeah.

-- I don't know. Twenty or thirty. I don't count, man. Things just happen.

-- How'd you start?

-- How do you think? Had a girlfriend. I also had a sidepiece (like everybody else), and was trying to keep it on the DL. The first time, I just got tired of the ex complaining. Asking: Where I was? Who she saw me with? So I lied. She believed me.

Eventually, I figured I could borrow money from her and not pay her back. Take things from her apartment and sell it off. I got a kick out of her looking for shit like she lost it. That was funny. She'd ask me to help her search her apartment. It took me everything to not bust out laughing. Then, she'd ask me about the money I owed her and I'd claim that I already paid her. You know, "Baby, what are you talking about? I paid you back last week." That shit had me.

I was broke back then. So when the sidepiece asked me to move in, I dumped the girl. When she asked why, I told her, "Cause I'm sick of you forgetting everything." Man, she couldn't stop crying.

Man, women are so clingy. They want all your time. But I don't want to hang out with their friends. I mean, if they want to hang out with my friends that's okay, but only on my terms. I got no time for a girl's friends. Yeah, I'll play the game. I'll be their 'friend' just long enough to get dirt. Women are so gullible. That's when I talk smack about their friends to her, and spread rumours to their pals. Can't have a girlfriend with anyone around them. She might sleep with one of them. That's my game. Cheating with my woman's friends is intense. You ever slept with your girl's friends?

-- No.

-- You're missing out buddy! The sidepiece I moved in

with, I slept with all her friends! Man, they all thought that she was beating me up and stealing my money. Like sex with me was charity. Man, I slept with her best friend, in her bed!

-- That's messed up man.

-- Yeah, probably. But I was young when I did that shit. I don't really do that anymore. Okay, I convinced one of my buddy's girlfriend to leave him for me. Then I dumped her. You know, "Bros before hoes." I heard that she had a mental breakdown. But, she was bad for my dude. I wouldn't have done that if I thought she was right for my dog Langston. What was her name again? I think it was Tanya.

-- So you mess with people you don't date?

-- Yeah. I don't have to even sleep with someone to mess with their head. That was just an example. You know, if I need some cash, messing with someone is easy. Just find a mark. You know, a fool who stands out. Become their friend. Let them share their secrets with you. Make up a crazy secret and tell them, so they think that you're mutually suffering. And then, "Hey Stevie, did you see my wallet?"

"No buddy, let me help you look for it. Oh, here it is."

"Thanks. Strange, I thought I had a bit more than this."

"Don't worry, I got the drinks tonight."

But it isn't always about money. Sometimes, I just want to mess with people.

-- Why?

-- I don't know. You get used to it. But, when you got a girl, a sidepiece and money, when you're comfortable with your life, you still need that adrenaline rush. Know what I mean?

I used to mess with these old neighbours I had. They would get a package delivered at their door, and I would steal it and watch them flip out for a few days. Like a week later, I would knock on their door and apologize. Explain that their package was delivered to me. The husband would get so pissed at whatever courier service they used. That shit was hilarious.

-- So there's more than one type of gaslighting?

-- Are you listening? You don't gas everybody. You gas people who become dependent on you. Or, you gas people who are weaker than you. I don't care about the type of gaslighting. I'm looking for targets. It's crazy, you're swimming in someone's head, but they don't know it. They might not even know you. But you're in their head. Isn't that crazy? You own real estate in someone's head!

You walk around and see people who you've messed with. And you know you've messed with that person. You stole money from that guy. You made that woman have a nervous breakdown. That grandpa takes heart medicine 'cause you fucked with him. Walking is different when you own real estate in all the people around you's heads.

You know that first girl, or boy you kissed and they kissed you back? (Sorry dude, I don't know what floats your boat.) How they got a permanent spot in your brain? That spot? I didn't have to kiss no virgins to get it. But I'm no narcissist, I'm an adrenaline junky. I look at a person like they're my mountain to climb. If I fall, I lose a bunch of friends, I might go to jail. All sorts of crazy stuff. Might as well die, know what I mean?

For instance, right now I'm dating this foreign girl. Beautiful as anything. She didn't have many friends, so it didn't take long to befriend them all. And I have tons of friends. I introduced her friends to mine. Set the single ones up on dates. Talk to her mother on the phone. Everyone loves me.

Right now, I'm just starting things. I'm telling her mother that she's acting strange. Private messaging her friends that she's being weird. That they should just keep an eye out.

I've been slowly taking money out of her bank account. Her pin is mad easy. I'm not taking out a lot. Just enough for her to be confused. Look at her bank statement and wonder why she took out that sixty bucks, or whatever. Make her have to apologize to her landlord 'cause her checking account was five dollars short on rent. Her landlord doesn't care. He finds her cute. But soon, he's at least going to be worried about her, or take advantage of her.

Meanwhile, I'm taking all her friends, and the ones I can't win over, I'm making them run away from her. By the time that I'm done, she's going to be begging mommy for a plane ticket home. But mommy's under my thumb too.

-- And you say you're not a psychopath?

-- Look, I don't get off killing people. People die sometimes, if you push them too hard, but I don't want that! How can the thing that I did float around in their head if they're dead?

-- People have died?

-- Yeah, a guy I knew committed suicide. That was fucked up. I told him it was all a bad joke and I'd get his job back for him, or help him find a better job. Dude was mad calm. Said, "Don't worry." So I didn't. Next day they found him overdosed on pills.

-- What did you do?

-- I laughed. What could I do? I said I was going to help the guy get his job back. It was a shitty job. But if he wanted it, I could have gotten him the exact shitty job he had. I thought it was funny, but then, I realized that he was the one that got away.

Narcissism? Narcissists are all like "Look at me. Look at me." But I'm like, "Don't look at me. Pay me no mind." And then, when you finally realize, you're all alone and you only have me – snip. I'm gone. Beautiful isn't it? I don't want you to look at me. I want to pull your strings. Then one. At a time. They all break. And you fall down.

Is that enough? You told me that if I helped you with your documentary, and told you everything, that I could go, right? You said I'm getting paid for this, right?

-- Yes, yes we did. And you've answered our questions. We just have a few more, if that's okay with you.

-- No problem.

-- I'm going to order some food. Would you be interested in having some steak?

-- Steak sounds good. What else do you want to know?

-- Do you have any rules?

-- Yeah. Tons. I love my friends. All of them. I collect friends. Most of them used to be someone else's friend. I might of stolen one or two. But they mean the world to me. They're like jewels. So, I try not to mess with them. There are exceptions. Like, Langston's ex, but I'm telling you there's something about her that bothers me.

I can't explain it. Tanya was cool. Ah! Whatever. How long for the food?

-- Probably ten more minutes.

-- Cool. What was I thinking. Oh! Other rules. Never hang out with someone that I've gassed afterwards. Even if they don't know that I was gaslighting them. No, that's not true. Sometimes it's funny. But I try to keep my distance. You know, I can't have someone I screwed over asking me weird questions about stuff. You can only keep up so many lies at one time. Lying is easy. Remembering those lies takes memorization. Sometimes, I keep notes on someone on my phone. You know, so that I can remember everything that I've said to them. Crazy, right? People think I'm looking at texts. Nope!

Everything's got rules. I mean, it sucks if they find out what you're doing. You don't want that. Then you have to go find new friends, or call everyone before they do. You know how much it sucks to call people and be like, "I heard that crazy girl was saying that I was messing with her. Crazy. Some people can't take responsibility for themselves. Always gotta blame someone. No, let her talk. You know how she is."

Seriously, it's tiring keeping that act up until you finish calling everyone. I'm not trying to do work. I'm creating art. I'm climbing a mountain. This ain't work.

Hey, can I get a beer with this steak?

-- No problem.

-- Awesome.

Have you ever climbed a mountain? Or gone on a hike up a mountain?

-- No, I don't really like heights.

-- You're missing out. Like I said, I'm an adrenaline junkie. I've climbed mountains. Sometimes, when you're half way up, you gotta go down a bit to find a better route, know what I'm saying? Same with gaslighting. When stuff like them realizing what's going on happens, you gotta go back two or three steps. You have to make sure all their old friends are still in your pocket. It's the least fun part of doing this shit.

Everything else is fun. You get that adrenaline rush 24/7. That's why it's so much better than climbing a mountain, or bungee jumping, or whatever. Bungee jumping, you get that rush for what? Five, six seconds? To be honest, cliff diving is better. You get the rush falling down, and then you have to make sure that you don't hit the rocks underwater. You don't feel safe until you get your head above water. After that, you can still drown, or crash against the cliff because of a wave. You're buzzing for like ten minutes, until you get back to your boat or the shore. Way better than bungee jumping.

So when are you guys going to release this documentary? You're going to blur my face and change my voice right? I don't need any trouble 'cause I helped you out. Also, can you tell me who told you about me? I'm just curious. I've probably burned the person so bad that getting revenge wouldn't be worth it.

Maybe I should write a book. Use a – what do they call it? A pseudonym, or an alias or something. Give it one of those self help-meets-Eastern philosophy names like the Tao of Gaslighting. Or Six Easy Ways to Fuck Up Someone's Life.

Man, I'm feeling tired. I know that we're doing this interview in a hotel room, but I shouldn't be getting sleepy, even if a bed is just over there.

-- My apologies. Let me answer all your questions and then I'll explain what is happening to you.

First, this documentary is for a very small and exclusive audience. Let's say it's a limited release. Let's say, the number of patrons for this film are such a small number, that you don't have to worry about your secret getting out. We're not going to blur your face or hide your voice.

You are probably noticing that you are having a hard time speaking now. Don't worry, you'll be fine. We just put a little something in your drink to help you rest a bit. Don't panic. If you follow our instructions no one is going to kill you. Maybe a few broken bones, but nothing a good doctor friend of mine and a few weeks in bed won't cure. Think of it as... climbing a... No, that doesn't work. White water rafting. An adventure, down a river. If you listen to your guide – that would be me – you'll be fine. Let's see, I can't tell you who told me about you. Well actually, I was looking for someone else, but your name kept popping up. No one person told me. I figured it out on my own.

Ever heard the saying, "Don't mess with someone, because you never know who they really are?" No? Oh well, you can't talk, can you? Just remember that saying for me would you? Oh yes, alias and pseudonym work, but my favourite is nom de plume.

Excuse me, can you hit stop on the camera? Let's not use our real names just in case. We have to pick them up from the rendezvous --

*The camera is shut off.*


II.

It started a few days ago. I only scan through emails on my phone. I hate the lack of connectivity everyone has. Staring at their phone. I'll check a map, or occasionally chat on social media, but I don't really check my emails until I get home from work.

So, I was checking my spam. Sometimes, things end up there. One subject line caught my eye, because they knew my full name. Most spammers use usernames. When I clicked on the email it had a weird message:

> Attention Langston James: You have been wronged.
>
> Dear Mr. James,
>
> My name is Edward. I was hired by my client to investigate a matter. Unfortunately, through my investigation, I've discovered that you too may be a victim of a particular perpetrator. I am contacting you to see if you are interested in learning how you've been wronged.
>
> If you are curious, send me a brief reply with Yes in the title, or in the body of the email. I'll call you to confirm things in a few days, if you are interested.
>
> Thank you, Mr. James. I hear that this is an important week at work for you. Good luck, and I look forward to meeting you in the near future.
>
> Sincerely,
>
> Edward.

I thought that it was strange that this guy Edward said he was going to call if I was interested. Did he really have my phone number? Weird. More to the point, this guy either knew that I was up for a promotion, or he was bluffing. It was obviously not spam, but was this guy trying to hustle me? I've been suckered before. But I was curious.

What the hell. I figured if it was a scam, "Edward" wouldn't have my number and nothing more would come of it. It was probably a high level bot. At worst, I would have to change my password.

My week went well. I've been dating one of my exes for the past couple months. This week we made some headway. We finally talked about why we broke up. I didn't get mad at her, and she was cool with my side of things.

At work, I got my promotion. It's a crappy job, but I moved up from carrying boxes to being part of their management trainee program. That's two dollars more an hour. The possibility of more shifts. I might be able to turn this into a career.

However, on Friday I received a call from an unlisted number.

"Hello?"

"Hello Langston? This is Edward. I emailed you earlier in the week." I didn't connect his name to the message right away. Plus, this guy had perfect English, but a super weird accent, maybe German. "Did you forget my email? The one about the investigation I am in the midst of? Also, did you get that promotion?"

Oh, this guy. The creepy email about me being a

victim. "I remember. Are you some sort of cop or private detective or something? How'd you get my number?"

"Let's just say that I'm a private investigator." Okay, weird. "A number of the victims – no I don't want to use the word victim – a number of the people who have been taken advantage of by the gentleman that I am investigating will be getting together tomorrow. Will you join us? You're actually friends with some of them. I'm not sure if you're a victim, but if you could come as support, that would be wonderful."

I was curious. "Who will I know there?"

"Robert will be visiting with us. Your girlfriend, is it Tanya?"

"Yeah, Tanya."

"Your old roommate James. A lot of the people there you probably won't know. But if you could come for your friends, that would be great."

I was in my studio apartment, sitting on my couch watching TV. Tanya and I had just started to mend things. It would probably cause problems if I didn't show up after being invited to support her. Plus, it had been a while since I saw James. I see Robert every other week. No big deal. But maybe we could all grab a beer after this weird meeting.

"Okay, where are we meeting?"

"At a conference hall just outside of town. I'm picking everyone up at the mall just west of your apartment."

"You're picking us up?"

"Yes, there's quite a lot of you. So I decided to rent a bus. That way no one can get lost." Man this guy is weird.

"Which entrance?" I asked.

"By the liquor store at 10 AM."

As I hung up, I stared at my TV. The whole thing sounded strange, but the mall is close to my apartment. It wouldn't be a big deal to go for a walk Saturday morning to grab breakfast in that neighbourhood. If Tanya and the guys were there I would stick around. I decided against telling Tanya that I was coming. If she wasn't sure about this, I didn't want her to show up just because she thought she should meet me. The whole thing felt unusual. She could decide for herself.

Somehow, I woke up around 9 the next day. I hadn't bothered to pull out the bed, and had just slept on the sofa. To be honest, that's what I usually do unless I have a guest. After a quick shower I put on a t-shirt, jeans, grabbed my things and threw on a jacket on my way out the door.

When I got to the mall entrance by the liquor store, a handful of my friends – some from my present, some from my past – let out a cheer. "Langy!" James yelled out the loudest.

Tanya was surprised to see me. She didn't know that Edward had contacted me as well. There were about sixteen of us there. I knew Zoe, Len, Rich, James, and Tanya. There was quite a variety of people. I noticed a senior couple, and a young girl, barely in her twenties. I guessed the rest were only slightly older than my group of friends.

A charter bus pulled up to the curb, shiny white with tinted windows hiding any view of the passengers. We gathered around the door and a man with a familiar voice stepped out and greeted us.

It was Edward. He was at least six-four. Dirty blond hair. Clean cut. Wearing a leisure jacket. He looked exactly how I imagined him over the phone.

"Greetings. Before you enter the bus I just have a few words." Edward cleared his voice and continued. "For your safety and mine, if you enter this bus, you will be asked to wear a blindfold, and to hand me your cell phone. I know, that sounds obscene, but everything will make sense when we reach our destination.

"Also, there are already some people on the bus. Some of them are sleeping – our other rendezvous spot was some miles away. Please do not disturb them. If you are okay with those two rules, please come in. You can sit anywhere you like. There should be enough seats for you to sit beside a friend, or by yourself if you do not know anyone here."

"What if we're uncomfortable with wearing a blindfold and going on a bus to God knows where?" someone chimed in.

Edward froze, probably for theatrical effect, before he responded.

"You're free to go home. Unfortunately, we don't have much time, but please make a decision that you will be happy with."

We all looked at each other. I didn't wake up early on my day off to go back home. I grabbed Tanya's hand, gave Edward my phone at the bottom of the steps, took two blindfolds from a box, and found seats for us.

Surprisingly, everyone who waited with us had the same mentality. I watched Edward put all of our phones in a small knapsack as people entered. Then he walked down the aisle like a flight steward. He watched while we slipped on the provided eye masks. A moment after my world went dark I heard the brakes hiss, and then I could feel the bus move. Classical music played at a low volume over the sound system.

Even in this bizarre circumstance, I knew something was off. Someone was missing. Then it hit me: Robert. He probably overslept. But this kind of thing was right up his alley. If it wasn't so elaborate, I would have sworn it was one of his pranks.

But for some reason, it didn't feel like a prank. I decided not to mess around. I would take today seriously.

I don't know how long the bus ride was. Maybe three quarters of an hour? I know we got on a highway, but couldn't tell how long we were on it. It was odd to discover that being blindfolded can mess with your sense of time. We could have ended up in another town, or just in the suburbs. When the bus finally stopped,

Edward got on the PA. "Ladies and gentleman, please awaken. We have reached our destination." After repeating himself three times he realized he had forgotten to tell us something. "My apologies," he added. "You are more than welcome to take off those blindfolds."

I let go of Tanya's hand, took off the blindfold, and looked around. We were parked in a big garage, or warehouse, or abandoned factory. Needless to say, there were no windows.

"Wonderful, you're all up." Edward seemed pleased. "This is our bus driver, Mike. He's going to show you where the washrooms are. We've ordered food, but there are some vending machines near the washrooms as well. After you've all freshened up, I shall meet you in the conference room. Please, for all our safety, do not try to figure out where we are."

Mike directed us towards a door, which led to a hallway with a small sitting area, vending machines, and washrooms. Tanya and I split up to use the washroom. I was the last guy out the Men's. No one was there. I saw a sign that said Conference Room 1 and headed towards it. Suddenly, I heard Mike's voice. "Mr. James! You're heading in the wrong direction!" I turned around and saw him by the door we had entered. "The room we're going to is on the other side." He smiled one of those customer service, beauty pageant smiles. It was just genuine enough that I smiled back and followed him.

We walked past the parked bus to another door. There

was a sign that said Conference Room 2. As Mike and I entered, Edward looked at us with relief. "Great! You found us. We've been introducing ourselves. Why don't you take your turn, Langston, since you are standing."

"Hi, my name is Langston. I went to school to study geography but ended up touring the world as a break dancer. Since then, I've been perpetually broke." A gentle wave of laughter greeted me. "Well, right now I work a soul sucking job in retail, but I just was promoted to manager trainee." I was surprised that everyone applauded. I felt welcomed. Tanya wasn't the only person smiling. "Well, that's me."

I manoeuvred to the empty seat beside Tanya, and sat down and listened to the last few introductions. Then Edward spoke.

"Hello everyone. It is a pleasure meeting you all face-to-face. Even though this is our first time together I feel as if I already know many of you. As some of you may have already guessed, my real name is not Edward, and I'm not from here. It's probably the accent that gives it away." We all laughed. None of us were surprised at this point.

"Obviously, Mike's name is not Mike either. However, our names never did matter. All of yours do. I lied to some of you." Edward looked directly at me. "I said that you should come to support your friends. That was not true. If you are here, you are a victim. Several of you asked me if I was a private detective. Let us just say that

I am a researcher. I do research for people who would prefer to keep my research a secret.

"A friend of a friend, someone who has nothing to do with the industry that I primarily work in, asked me to answer a question for them. Unfortunately, as I found the answers to questions they had, all of your names began to appear." Edward pushed his hand through his hair. "I could have kept it all to myself, but I am a gentleman who believes that people should have free will to decide their futures. If I did not contact you all, I would not be able to sleep at night."

What the hell? Was I a victim of some organized crime scam? Was this guy going to tell us that our identifications have been stolen? Even he looked uneasy here.

Edward sighed and then continued. "I am going to show you all a short, let's say, documentary, then some files. Afterwards, I would like us all to come to a consensus. Yes? Mike, shut off the lights and play the video please."

A projection screen came down in the front of the room and a video started.

There he was. Robert. It was definitely him. Wearing his favourite dark brown leather jacket and what looked like a new outfit.

My left hand covered my mouth as my right squeezed Tanya's. No one spoke. We listened for forty minutes as he explained what he had done to us. When he said those numbers, "Twenty or thirty," I counted the heads in the room. There were twenty-six of us. Edward had found all of Rob's living victims. He probably flew some of us in.

I knew that Tanya had slept with Rob. He told me that she threw herself at him a week after we broke up. She admitted sleeping with him when we got back together. I didn't realize it was a planned goal of his, to manipulate her into sleeping with him. How was I so gullible?

I suddenly remembered all the old trinkets and small items I used to have that had disappeared over the years. Some of them were valuable. There he was, on video, saying that Tanya was the only time that he screwed me over, but this bastard robbed me too!

Around us, I could hear crying. The young woman who came on the bus with us was sobbing loudly – she was probably Robert's new girlfriend. The senior couple tried their best to stifle their moans in their handkerchiefs. As Tanya squeezed my hand tighter and tighter everyone stared at the screen.

We watched as the drugs Edward gave Robert started to take effect. That German accent echoed in the conference room. "Ever heard the saying, 'Don't mess with someone, because you never know who they really are?' No? Oh well, you can't talk, can you? Just remember that saying for me would you? Oh yes, alias and pseudonym work, but my favourite is nom de plume."

There was some rustling as someone took the camera

off the tripod. Moments later, the video ended and Mike turned on the lights.

We were all in shock. Probably for various reasons of our own. We all had different types of relationships with Rob, I imagined. We were friends, lovers, partners, neighbours, business partners of his. No. We all had the same relationship with Robert.

Edward handed each of us our file. The things stolen and pawned off, Robert's signature on deliveries meant for us, photos, phone records, bank statements with highlighted transactions, documents. Edward's research was thorough. He knew who Robert had taken advantage of, how, and when.

We were given ten minutes to look over the files and then Edward addressed us. This time he pulled a chair to the front. "So." He stared down at his shoes and then continued. "I've known killers. I've been friends with killers. But I've never met someone so maniacal and cold in my entire life. That's why I gathered you all here. The question is what do you want to do?"

He stood up, paced for a bit with his head down, then stopped and faced us. "First, this isn't some stupid Korean vengeance film where you get to cut off limbs or something. That's utterly ridiculous."

"So what would you do?" yelled James from the back.

Edward sat back down in front of us. Scratched his head for a second and shared his thoughts. "The thing that struck me when I interviewed him was that idea that he owned real estate in peoples' minds. This is your chance to evict him from up there. I figure that you have three choices.

"One: I give all this evidence to a contact of mine who is a police officer. But to be honest, a lot of these are summary offences. You would all probably have to be interviewed, or testify in court. It would be a lot of paper work for maybe a big fine?

"Two: You do nothing. Take home the knowledge that all those things you thought were missing, and all those times you were lied to, were real. Now that you know that you are not crazy, you can seek help.

"Three: I'm wary of telling you this, but Robert is in this building." Everyone breathed in at once and froze at this, and Edward gave us a moment to digest it. "If you wish," Edward resumed, "I will give you each five minutes with him. Want to scream at him? Punch him? Anything within reason. I promised him that nothing would happen to him that a doctor couldn't fix. In turn, he has promised not to report any of you."

"How can you guarantee that?" someone near the front asked.

"He knows that I can find him. He knows the type of friends I have. In my business, my word is my bond.

"Why don't you all speak amongst yourselves. I want a consensus. Think about how you can all evict this man from the real estate in your head, yes? If you look to the left there are cookies, fruit, sandwiches, juice, pop, beer and a few wine coolers. Help yourselves. I will leave you for fifteen minutes. You all remember where the washrooms are? Great. Mike?"

Mike was leaning against the front door. He opened it and the two disappeared. I grabbed a beer for myself, a wine cooler for Tanya, and a pop for James. When I got back to our seats Tanya had brought over some sandwiches. The six of us who had a past together gathered. We were joined by the young woman who I thought was Robert's current girlfriend.

"So what do you think?" I asked our group of jurists.

"I think we go to the cops," James said. "It's the most work, but it's the right thing to do --"

"Honestly," I cut in, "I'm okay leaving things as they are. Now that I know what's been going on, I think I can make serious strides in therapy. There was always something stopping me from gaining more self confidence. Maybe this --"

"I just want to scream in his face. Fuck him. I knew something was strange. All my friends were asking me funny questions. Fuck him. I want to put all the shit he said in a bucket and pour it all on him." There was a power behind the words of this petite young woman. I saw some people in other groups look up as she spoke.

About ten minutes into our time, the grandpa walked to the front of the room. "Excuse me, ladies and gentle persons," he began. He spoke quietly, but as he spoke our volume dissipated. "I'm going to suggest that we have a vote now. If it's close between any of the choices we can talk it out, but if one choice is obvious, it's obvious. Does anyone have paper?"

No one had brought paper with them.

"Okay, we'll raise hands. Who wants to call the cops?"

No one raised their hands.

"What were the other two? Oh yes, who wants five minutes alone with him?"

All of our hands rose.

"I guess I didn't have to remember the last one." We all laughed. A guy who was on the bus before my group boarded left the room to get Edward.

"I have heard your decision," Edward announced. "I will take one of you at a time to see Robert. When you're finished, you will be sent to the bus with Mike, and asked to put your blindfold back on."

"Can two of us go in at the same time?" Tanya asked.

"Sure. I'm going to be in there to make sure none of you go too far. That's all I have to say. Who wants to go first?"

The guy who went to find Edward outside the conference room volunteered. After about three minutes, Edward reappeared. "Who's next?"

The room slowly emptied. Sometimes Edward came back in two minutes. Other times it was the full five minutes. Eventually, only Tanya and I remained. When Edward came we stood up together. The three of us walked out the door we had entered. Past the bus. Into the hallway with the washroom. Down the hallway to Conference Room 1.

When we got there Robert was in rough shape. Sitting on a chair. Tied up. Someone had punched him. You could see a footprint on his chest. You could smell urine on him. Someone had pissed on him. Tanya looked at me. Neither one of us could get joy from someone else's pain. We pulled up two chairs beside him and started to talk.

"Hey Robbie, you okay?" Tanya asked.

"I'm okay. I think I got a cracked rib, but no big deal. How are you guys? I didn't know you got back together?"

"Yeah, it's been a couple months now. Tee private messaged me on Twitter and we started talking. Crazy, isn't it?"

"You know I tapped that Langston."

"Yeah, I know. I'm not a virgin either."

"She's not good enough for you --"

"No, I'll be the judge of that from now on. We don't want to see you ever again," I explained to Rob, "but take care of yourself."

Tanya stood up. She reached for my hand. I rose too. She stood on the tips of her toes and I bowed down to her as our lips met.

This is what she wanted to show Robert when she asked Edward if two people could see him together: us happy. Unbreakable. Yeah we both fucked up the last time. We forgave one another. He could no longer burden us. We walked out hand in hand. Walked to the bus. Found two seats together, put on our eye shades and fell asleep holding hands.

I awoke to Edward shaking my shoulder. We were the last people on the bus. Edward smiled at the two of us. "Remember, only you own the real estate in your mind," he said. As I got up, I shook his hand. Tanya hugged him. Mike gave us our cell phones as we stepped outside. Waiting there were James, Zoe, Len and Robert's ex.

"So what should we do?" James asked.

"Well, the liquor store is right there," I pointed in front of me.

"And my boyfriend's shitty apartment is just around the corner," Tanya observed with a smile. "We have a lot to celebrate. I want to celebrate. Let's celebrate."

III.

I really like this Irish pub. The food is good. The booths are private. You can hang out by the bar with the girls and no one bothers you. Everyone is friendly. It's a great place to unwind after a tough week at work.

I was in a booth in the back, waiting for a guest. I was sipping a Guinness and had just ordered sweet potato fries with chipotle mayo when I heard a voice.

"Sorry, are you Miss Sparrow?" A man towered over me. I stood up to shake his hand.

"Mr. Guttenburg?" I asked.

"Yes, that is I." He turned towards the waitress. "Miss,

can you get me an espresso? Thank you."

Our server left and the two of us sat down.

"So you work in advertising, Miss Sparrow?"

"Yes."

"Nothing like the work your grandfather does," he said with a warm smile. "So why do I have the pleasure of meeting you today?"

"Papa and I were having our regular weekly phone call, and one of my ex-boyfriends came up. He was a bit younger than me, but Papa liked him almost as much as I did. He's the only person I've dated who wasn't afraid of Papa. They would go to plays, sports, have drinks together." I couldn't help smiling. Mr. Guttenburg was also smiling. "He was perpetually broke, but he was a great guy. But maybe two years into our relationship, all these rumours started swirling around him. We got into a lot of fights. Eventually, we broke up."

"Did you at least remain friends?"

"No. I was so angry with him that I slept with one of his friends. He blocked my email address… The thing is, after we broke up, I learned that most of the rumours were bullshit. If I had known the truth, we still might have broken up, but I sure wouldn't have slept with his friend. There might have been a chance to try again, eventually." I watched Mr. Guttenburg's smile dissolve as he listened to my story.

"Anyway, I just want to see how he's doing. Has he been eating? Is he happy? That sort of thing."

"Did you bring the papers that I requested?"

"Yes, I have his old email address, phone number, pictures, everything I could find." I handed Mr. Guttenburg an expanding file folder, which he placed in his attaché case.

"Usually, this would be the last time I would see a client," he explained. "I would deliver my findings via the dark net, or if it was something this informal, via Snapchat. But as you are the granddaughter of Mr. Sparrow, I shall meet you again next week. Same bar?"

As he finished speaking, our orders arrived. Mr. Guttenburg downed his espresso and placed way too much cash on the table. Before I could give him some change, he smiled and left.

I was with Lexi and Shawnette at the bar the next Friday. Lexi and Shawnette work for the law firm next to the ad agency I'm at. We had just ordered a second round when Mr. Guttenburg entered, wearing a blue suit and red tie. The girls undressed him with their eyes as he walked towards us at the bar.

"Miss Sparrow, ladies," he said. I watched as my two girlfriends melted in his hands. He turned to me. "I'm happy to say I found all the information that you wanted. I'll grab a booth in the back so that we can have a bit of privacy."

As he walked away Shawnette demanded, "Who is he? And is he single?"

"He's a friend of my grandfather's. If you want to know if he's single, I'll ask for you," I teased. I had a sip of my martini, got off the stool, and followed Mr. Guttenburg to a booth in the rear of the pub.

When we were both seated, he began with his usual smile. "Great news: Mr. James is doing well. He doesn't know it, but his boss is interested in having him apply for a manager trainee role. He's stopped dancing, but now that he has a steady job he's moved. His apartment is smaller, but it's much nicer than the place he was in when you two dated.

"I was pretty interested in the rumours you heard about him. The reason why your breakup was so tumultuous. Do you know a Mr. Dixon?"

"Yeah, he's the one I slept with."

"Hmm… That would make some sense. A fair amount of people around Mr. Dixon seem to have had some bad luck."

"Really?"

"Most of it small. They have had to cancel credit cards, or debit cards multiple times because they lost them. Small thefts. They have reported missing items. That sort of thing.

"But there are some bigger tragedies too. One of his friends overdosed on prescription drugs. A neighbour had a pretty severe heart attack. If you don't mind, I would like to look further into this. Your grandfather suggested that I spare no expense in my investigation.

But you might be satisfied with what I have --"

"No, if you're curious about Robert, dig deeper. If my Papa trusts your judgement so do I."

"Here is a list with Mr. James' new number, his current email address, his social media --"

"What am I going to do with this?" I asked as I grabbed the sheet of paper and slipped it into my purse.

"Be brave. You don't have an Instagram or Twitter account yet. Sign up. Like his photos. Private message him. Say hi. Apologize for your side of things. Tell him what you told me last week."

"But it's been nearly two years."

"You were together for two years as well. The worst thing that could happen is he says no, or blocks you. But what's the best thing that could happen?" Mr. Guttenburg left me with a great question. I started to feel warm inside.

"You know, my girlfriends were wondering if you're single," I informed him.

"Unfortunately, I don't date friends of my clients." He cleared his throat. "I hate lies, but you are going to have to tell them a small lie for me. Tell them that I just got engaged."

"Why?" I asked.

"No ring." Mr. Guttenburg showed me his left hand with a smile.

He stood up and headed towards the front exit. As he passed the bar, he whispered something to Lexi and Shawnette. I watched from the back as they both laughed.

The next time I saw him, his name would be Edward. Langston would be with me. We would be heading on a journey to see Robert Dixon for the last time.

I hear Robert's doing fine now. After he left town, he found a pretty good job. He doesn't hurt people anymore.

Langston and I are doing great. He moved in with me. He was just promoted to shift manager. I'm really proud of him. Papa took him fishing last week to celebrate.

-- No. He doesn't know that Papa and I were behind that Saturday.

## Dane Swan

Dane Swan was born in Bermuda and moved to Canada in his late teens. A classically-trained musician and a veteran of slam poetry stages across North America, his poetry and essays have appeared in numerous print and online journals. He has published two collections of poetry with Guernica Editions, *Bending the Continuum* (2011), and *A Mingus Lullaby* (2016), a finalist for the 2017 Trillium Book Award for Poetry.

## The Man Who Remembered the Moon
David Hull

He says it's gone. They say it never existed.
"Thoroughly satisfying." *The Globe and Mail*
"A beautifully executed, hypnotic shape-shifter." Christine
Fischer Guy, author of *The Umbrella Mender*

## Metaphysical Dictionary
Svetlana Lilova

"This sly, whimsical debut collection by Toronto poet Svetlana
Lilova is not much more than pocket-sized, but its poetic
reach is expansive… At their best, these epigrammatic gems
resonate profoundly." *The Toronto Star*

## Personal
Dave Green

Intimate, raw, and intensely personal: photos from the road,
the tavern - and the motel room too.

## You Call This Home
Joan Lane

"Keep on writing; your day will come. I hate to think of all that
talent going to waste." So said renowned Canadian novelist
Edward McCourt in 1957 about Joan Lane's stories. Sixty years
later, that day arrives with this posthumous collection.

**DUMAGRAD**
*a city of words*

*Available at dumagrad.com, at Amazon, and at
many fine indie bookstores.*